RICABAR'S
Deathwish

Humberto Garcia

author HOUSE

AuthorHouse™
1663 Liberty Drive
Bloomington, IN 47403
www.authorhouse.com
Phone: 833-262-8899

Published by AuthorHouse 09/19/2022

ISBN: 978-1-6655-7125-8 (sc)
ISBN: 978-1-6655-7124-1 (e)

Library of Congress Control Number: 2022917346

As the night dragged on at an excruciatingly slow pace, Ricabar Dane prayed that his body would somehow find a way to give up working and that he would quietly and peacefully slip into a permanent slumber. He was tired of being confined to the solitude of his dark and lonely cell though he knew he had earned his ticket to admission to wherever men like him went after their lives were gone. Lying on his bed fully awake he looked in every direction around him, but the view never changed. Complete darkness is all he could see. Not only did the complete absence of light bring him to despair but the lack of any sound as well compounded his inability to fall asleep. On top of this the irritation he felt only made the problem worse. Not being able to sleep drove his mind to thoughts of suicide and different ways he could accomplish it. However, nothing in the small cell he called home provided any assistance. A metal bed that did not move with a mattress lacking sheets provided no comfort. A steel commode attached to the wall and personal items, which could serve as tools of death were of no help. There was nothing he could use to bring an end to his misery. His lack of creativity in achieving his untimely death created a desire to yell out in anger but he knew this would only force further sanctions upon him by the uncaring guards who ruled the night. He wondered how it was that he had not gone insane after all this time in solitary confinement. To him, the prospect of death seemed far more favorable than being alive and confined to a prison cell knowing he would never be released.

To add to his frustration and inability to sleep, he thought about the uncertainty and time-consuming process of the appellate court system, which held his fate in its midst. Ricabar had spent eight years on death row at the Allen B. Polunsky Unit of the Texas Department of Criminal Justice, which operates the state's prisons and where the cruelest and most dangerous murderers are confined as they await their appointment with the grim reaper. Ricabar was one of those deemed to be deserving of the ultimate penalty but his turn in the death chamber, twice scheduled, had been turned back by the courts as his appeal was considered. Though he had not vocalized it to his lawyers, over the last two years he had come to grips with the notion that the punishment imposed on him was well deserved and should be carried out without further delay. Now, there was no longer any justification for trying to avoid his fate, he thought, as he had come full circle to admit that he was undoubtedly responsible for the death of his victim. For the first six years on death row he had denied to everyone, including his mother, that he had committed the atrocity for which he was convicted by a Bexar County jury. He had also been insistent in telling his lawyers he was innocent, and everything should be done by them to spare him the death penalty the jury said was warranted. He had consistently blamed someone else for the crime but, spending his nights and days reading hundreds of books, including the Bible, his will had begun to break down. He had convinced himself that asking for forgiveness before he died was far more noble than to insist on hanging on to a lie that would surely foreclose any mitigation of his condemnation by the Lord. Now that he had recognized and embraced his guilt he had grown eager to enter the permanent darkness.

Rotating from his right to his left side in an effort to begin his slumber proved unsuccessful over the several hours that he made his attempt. He usually would not fall asleep until three to four hours after he hit his prison bed but tonight it had been six and he felt no closer to sleep than when he laid down. Admittedly the bed in his cell was not the most comfortable and it was not big enough to accommodate his six-foot six frame, but he had gotten accustomed to its inadequacies and he had been able to drift off into dreamland for years. Tonight seemed different. His sense of guilt had never been so intense. Perhaps this was part of the punishment that he so justly deserved, he thought. Indeed, agonizing over the death, which he had caused with his bare hands, was now worse than the actual physical confinement. His anxiety forced him to reflect upon his childhood and eventually to the events leading up to his unspeakable crime.

Ricabar was a child of the streets, a product of the East side of San Antonio. Although he lived with his mother in one of the several housing projects built in the sixties, he spent most of his time with some friends in the streets, looking for vulnerable places to burglarize or sometimes rob at gunpoint at the young age of 7. The little money they reaped from their misdeeds was spent on cheap highs from aerosol paint cans and glues. By the time he was ten, he had dropped out of school, but his mother never noticed as she was constantly spaced out on cocaine or heroin. Sometimes he was the one who supplied her candy. This way, he could keep her from knowing of his activities. While she was high she never asked him what he was up to.

He and his boys had started robbing small shops in the neighborhood and then moved up to bigger places, such as liquor and convenience stores on the west side of town when they could get hooked up with a car, stolen or borrowed. The fact they had not been caught during any of the robberies made them feel untouchable and kept their criminal string going. When they could not take money from their victims they took items they could sell to willing fences in the neighborhood. They never reaped more than a few hundred dollars each time, but this was enough to buy the drugs that took them away from the reality of the dreadful lives they led in their world. School and work were the farthest things from Ricabar's mind and those of his friends.

Living in a home where the only person who could provide any supervision was a mother who was constantly absent, either physically or by being high on drugs, made it easy for him to roam the streets and fill his life with mischief. He was first lured to a miscreant life by his friends but by the time he was 15, he was the one leading a wave of crime in the streets in San Antonio. He had convinced his fellow delinquents that they had not been caught because of his leadership and cunning methods. Despite the numerous times they illegally took someone's possessions, they had never caused any physical harm to any of their victims. This, he contended, was the reason little attention was paid to their crimes. Indeed, sometimes the victims would not even call the police to report their losses.

Ricabar had no other family besides his mother. The few relatives his mother told him about had already discarded her because of her habits. She had lost any chance she had to get them to take Ricabar into their homes. He was fine with this, as he preferred his unfettered freedom. Even if they had taken him in, he would just have run away and done as he pleased. In his mind, being alone was much better than trying to please some aunt or uncle just so he could have a place to sleep at night. He rarely thought about his father, though he knew who he was. However, he had never met him and knew little about him. He was aware that he was a student from Haiti when he met his mother and had a brief relationship that produced him, but he knew nothing of his whereabouts. He assumed he had gone back to Haiti, but he really did not care. He knew that his name was Ricardo Baron Duvries but he had never seen any document with his name or any picture of him. His mother had told him that she did not record his name as the father when he was born. She had been angered by his denial of paternity and because he left her when she told him she was pregnant. Despite being angry with his father, Medita Dane created a name for her son by combining the first four letters of his father's first name with the first three of his middle name and then gave him her last name. This, she felt, was a way to remind her that even though she was angry, she was hopelessly in love with him and could hold on to a piece of him. She had told Ricabar this made him unique.

Though Medita was right about her son having a unique name, she never really gained a full understanding of how unique he truly was, as she never paid any attention to Ricabar's report cards when he was attending school. Neither had she understood the results of her son's I.Q. tests when he was five. She conveniently assumed that he was sharp enough to care for himself so that she could avoid feeling guilty about leaving him alone while she sold her body to support her habit. Ricabar never understood the meaning of the report cards or test results either. All he knew was that seeing and understanding the real world around him came easy. He could analyze and comprehend the situations he faced daily, especially when committing crimes. He had a keen appreciation of the dangers he and his friends encountered and made decisions quickly about how to handle and avoid the consequences of their deeds. He could instantly tell how much money they had taken by one quick glance of the bills. He would say to his friends how much and then tell them to count all the ones, tens and twenties they had grabbed. He was never wrong.

Medita had enjoyed a promising life before she resorted to prostitution to survive. When she met Ricardo, they both talked about the wonderful life they would enjoy upon his completion of his studies. In fact, he had already convinced her to return with him to Haiti right after graduation. He told her that he would have a very good job with the government waiting for him. Medita loved the idea of being the wife of a government official. His charm and bravado painted a picture of political and financial power they would enjoy in his native land. Though this was enough to convince her to go with him back to Haiti, he poured it on by telling her she would likely be the first lady of Haiti as he was sure he would eventually run for president of his country. She was eager to go and was anxiously awaiting his graduation, but something went terribly wrong. As soon as Ricardo learned she was pregnant, his attitude changed. He accused her having a sexual relationship with another man and denied that he fathered the expected child even though he had no proof and Medita vehemently denied being unfaithful. Nevertheless, Ricardo stopped seeing her and refused to take her calls. When she tried to visit him at his apartment, he refused to answer the door despite her pleas. Medita could only surmise that her pregnancy had caused Ricardo to change his views about her and the prospects of having her join him in Haiti. Immediately upon graduation, Ricardo fled the U.S. without telling Medita. When she found out he left, Medita tried to get an abortion but the doctor told her she was too far along, and it would be too dangerous, and it was illegal. Distraught and abandoned, Medita also contemplated suicide. She gave up on that notion once the kicks inside her became stronger and more frequent. She never came close to any actual attempt. Her fear of pain and dying were too much of a deterrent.

Shortly after giving birth to Ricabar, Medita turned to drugs to console her emotional destruction. It is a wonder that Ricabar survived his infancy with his mother distracted by her depression and reliance on drugs. He was left alone for long periods of time and when she was around, she tried feeding Ricabar adult food. Sometimes she would leave him with a neighbor. Only then would Ricabar get the attention and care he needed. As much as she tried to be a mother to him, Ricabar rarely saw motherly love.

Medita attempted several jobs to get by but when she could not keep a job because of her drug use, she decided that selling herself was the only choice. Very little of the money she earned went to feed or clothe her son as most was used to feed her habit. That no one ever reported her to the child welfare authorities was a stroke of luck she did not deserve.

By the time he was three, Ricabar had learned to fend for himself. He was able to navigate through the kitchen and be creative with what was available in the refrigerator and pantry to feed himself. Though she never asked him, Ricabar would sometimes fix his mother a meal when she returned from tricking. She knew she was not worthy of his kindness, but she saw it made Ricabar feel good about himself. His demonstration of independence at such a young age was both amazing and scary in her view. She nevertheless did nothing to discourage her son's behavior as it meant she could spend more time prostituting herself. This meant more money to support her habit. It also meant she would spend less time lamenting the loss of her lover.

Though Ricabar was truly a gifted child, having to look out for himself in the absence of supervision from his mother, made him resentful and defiant of authority. When he was just over eight years old, he stopped showing up to school in the third grade although he managed to fool his mother into thinking that he was still attending classes. He managed to maintain the deception through what would have been his seventh grade. He would have been able to continue his ruse but at age 13, he got careless and was arrested for shoplifting a CD player from an electronic store and his mother had to show up to the juvenile detention facility to try to gain his release. The juvenile probation officer assigned to his case mentioned to her that he had contacted the school and he was told he had not been a student at any school for over four years. His mother was quite dismayed but chose not to make a big deal about it, as she did not want the authorities to look at her more closely. Before Ricabar could be taken to face the judge, he talked to the probation officer and offered to pay the store for the player even though he would not be keeping it. When the officer approached the prosecutor with the offer, the prosecutor balked at the prospect of seeing any money from the unemployed and truant boy but was impressed with the unsolicited offer. He felt he would challenge Ricabar by giving him only twenty-four hours to come up with the money. The next morning, Ricabar showed up at the prosecutor's office with the eighty dollars in cash. When the prosecutor asked him where he got the money, Ricabar unabashedly stated it was not part of the deal to reveal the source of his funds. The prosecutor laughed but took the money and said he would dismiss the charges. He assured Ricabar that if he found out that he had committed a crime to obtain the money, he would come down hard on him. What the prosecutor didn't know was that Ricabar and his friends had robbed a liquor store on the city's west side the night before and secured the funds, which would lead to his liberation. However, Ricabar had designated himself as the get-away-driver so that the conspicuousness of his six feet two-inch frame would not give the store attendant something to point out to the police. If that were to happen, the word would certainly get back to the prosecutor and he would be in greater trouble. The crime remained unsolved.

His brief encounter with the justice system did nothing to deter his criminal behavior. It did not take him long to plan other heists with his friends. Having gone through the system unscathed gave him confidence he could cheat the man. At that time, he did not consider that even a genius could get careless at the wrong time.

In the years following his arrest, Ricabar and his friends planned and executed numerous other robberies across the city. They were now using Halloween masks to hide their identities from the security cameras and they made sure each crime took only seconds to complete. Avoiding capture was always a factor in Ricabar's cunning plans so the details of their getaway were meticulous. Their take was never more than a few hundred dollars, but it was enough for all of them to pay for the basic necessities. Ricabar used a good portion of his share to supply his mother with drugs. Though she knew her son did not have a job, she never questioned the source of his money. As long as she could get her high, her son was free to do as he pleased. Their crime spree continued until Ricabar was 19. He finally got busted for the crime that brought him to this prison. Before he could replay the details of his gravest crime, a familiar dream sequence returned as he had finally fallen asleep.

In the scene, Ricabar was walking the dark hall of a building unknown to him. As he walked the hallway trying to find a way out, brief seconds of light would appear in front of him. Each time a light would appear, a person without a face would reach out to him and touch his body. Ricabar would swing his arm wildly at the figure but never made contact and the person disappeared. After several seconds passed, another light would shine and again a person without a face would appear and touch him. The hands would quickly move from his chest, then down and around to his buttocks. When the hand rubbed across his crotch, Ricabar tried to yell out but no sound came out of his opened mouth. Again, he swatted at the figure unsuccessfully. When the light and the person appeared for the third time, Ricabar reached for the person's neck and this time he felt his large hand grab the person's neck. Feeling something in his hand, he lifted the person off the floor and brought him closer to his face, so he could decipher who it was that was tormenting him. The light got brighter and as he brought the person's face closer to his, he saw an image of his own face, but it had no eyes. In their place, black holes seemed to look at him and he quickly let go of the person as he tried to scream. He awakened to realize he had revisited the same dream of many a night he had spent in his lonely cell. He tried to calm his heavy breathing and wiped his sweaty palms as he re-accommodated his enormous body on the tiny bed.

He realized he had only been asleep for minutes when he was interrupted by the recurrent nightmare. This is one of the reasons he had so much trouble going to sleep. Though he was tired and needed to sleep, his mind resisted the notion of dozing off and allow the demons to visit and torment him. Once he slowed his breathing and relaxed his body, he resumed his efforts to sleep. He had no clock in his cell but Ricabar could tell he had many hours before the daylight would return. In that time, his thoughts wandered looking for a solution to his dilemma.

As he lay in bed trying desperately to fall asleep, he could not help but reflect on all the offenses he had committed and the people whom he had deprived of their hard-earned money. Up until his arrest for the capital crime he now faced, he had not hurt any of them physically, but he nevertheless felt a tremendous sense of guilt and embarrassment. While captive in his cell, he slowly began to realize just how much intelligence and resourcefulness he had wasted. Indeed, he came to understand how he had used his God-given talents for the wrong purposes. He spent many agonizing hours imagining the great things he could have accomplished if his vision of the world had been different growing up. It would have been easy to blame his shortcomings on his mother and her lack of affection and attention, but that meant he had not grown up and matured. Time in prison made him accept responsibility for his own demise. It was because he had accepted his fate as that of his own making that he prayed every day and night seeking God's forgiveness. He tried using his prayers to atone for his misdeeds, but this brought him little solace. It frustrated him because he felt he needed to do more than pray to feel appropriately punished and make up for everything he had done to others. By now he had arrived at the point where he could accept that the only way to achieve atonement for his transgressions was to allow the state to carry out the death sentence against him. To this end, he had advised his lawyers that he no longer wanted them to pursue any appeals on his behalf. He wrote to them and very explicitly recognized that his execution was justified, and they should allow the system to impose the judgment handed down by the jury.

After he had written to his lawyers, he began to think that it would not be enough for another man to take his life away. In his mind this would not make him suffer for his sins and suffering was what he felt he needed to experience lest he remain laden with the guilt of sin for eternity. He thought execution by his Lord himself would be the only way to achieve complete atonement. It was this thought that drove him to pray every night that God come to him in the middle of the night and whisk him away from life on Earth. Then he began to wonder if this was just a foolish notion grown in his selfish mind. Was this the easy and cowardly way out? He assured God in his prayers that he was not afraid of pain so if the manner of death came with violence and pain, he would consider it justified and right. The nights of prayer continued for months with no sign of response. His commitment to the notion of being taken away by God himself grew stronger every night. In fact, he now began to think of the manner of his death. It did not matter how. So long as he knew God was acting as his executioner, his Lord would realize that Ricabar understood his life was being taken to pay for the one he took, and that meant justice was done.

His prayers were accompanied by ideas of how his life should come to an end. There could be a massive lightning strike, which only targeted his cell, he wondered. Or, there could be a rain of caustic and deadly chemicals or perhaps a poison in the water, which only affected his body. During the nights dominated by insomnia, many ideas crept into his mind, but he finally settled on one method. He felt the best and most dramatic way would be for his cell to be infiltrated by a thick mysterious mist, which would briefly awaken him from his slumber and then slowly choke him to death as he realized he was now paying the ultimate prize for all his sins.

When nothing came despite all his prayers, he began to think he was not the only one housed in this prison who deserved this punishment. What about all those who had also taken a life? Shouldn't they be taken as well even if they held no remorse for their crimes like he had? Yes, he thought. There was no reason to keep them locked up and away from civilization. Justice demanded that man rid himself of all those proven unworthy of life on this world. As he pondered this notion, he also thought about those who had committed crimes but had not been brought to justice. Should they not be also be made to pay for their sins? That would mean countless of people who could be subjected to the same fate, he thought. Yes, it was time to clean up the world and he felt responsible for leading the effort to convince God of his plan for eradication of the wicked.

On the third night of his eighth year on death row, Ricabar was approaching the much-needed sleep he longed for when he began to hear strange noises within his twelve by twelve jail cell. First, he heard what he thought were chains clinking against each other followed by scratches of fingernails against the cement walls. He wanted to convince himself that it was probably a mouse, but it would have to be a fairly sizable rodent to make that noise, he thought. They were followed by momentary silence. Then the tapping on the walls began, followed by sounds of wind hitting the ceiling of the cell. How could that be, Ricabar wondered silently? Was there a draft invading the cell which his senses could not detect?

When the noises persisted in the total darkness of his cell and the volume intensified, Ricabar began to get scared. He shouted, "Who's there?"

He raised his head thinking it would help him discover the source of the noises, but the impermeable darkness provided no clues. He got no response to his inquiry. When a chill ran through his back, he jumped off the bed and began to extend his hands to see if he could feel anything. There was no light switch in the cell as the lights were controlled by the switches at the guard's station and he had nothing that would provide any help to his blindness. The monster of a man was beginning to feel a dreadful fear.

"Is somebody in here?" he shouted to try again to figure out what the source of the noises was, but there was no response either. He swung his arms in a vain attempt to hit whoever might be in the room. This produced no answers to allay his fears.

As he stood frozen by the fear next to his bed, a light began to grow from the floor and slowly expand within the cell and move up toward the ceiling.

"Somebody jacking with me?" he shouted in despair. "Who's jacking with me?" he repeated.

The silence frightened him more. Surely somebody in the next cells must have heard him, he thought, but no other voice punctured the darkness of the night. He made his way toward the small window on the door to his cell and peered out, but he could see nothing, and the hall way was devoid of any sound. He thought that the light enveloping the cell would exit through the small window of the door but strangely, it did not leak into the hallway.

When he turned back to see his cell now fully lit by the unusual light, a figure began appearing in the middle of the room. Ricabar closed and opened his eyes repeatedly in attempt to clear his vision before he realized that there was a man present in the cell with him, but he could not make out the figure as the glow of the light around the figure distorted all features.

"Who are you?" he shouted. "How did you get into my cell?"

The figure moved slowly toward him but Ricabar saw no feet moving and heard no steps on the floor as it got within inches of his face.

"Ricabar. Don't you recognize me?" the mysterious figure asked in a thick Mexican accent and with a wry smile. Following the question, the figure moved back and began coming down. His feet were now resting on the floor of the cell and Ricabar could tell the man was much shorter as Ricabar was now looking down at him.

For a moment the sound of the figure's voice seemed familiar but Ricabar could not get a clear view of his face because of the light. His memory could not produce a name to go with the voice he heard. "I don't know you", he shouted. "You need to get out of my cell! How'd you get in here anyway?"

The figure shook his head as if disappointed and then softened the glow around his face to reveal identifiable features. As soon as Ricabar gazed at the face made clearer by the dimming of the light, Ricabar jumped back and yelled, "Jesus!"

"No, but I know him personally", the figure said with a snicker while placing his hand on Ricabar's shoulder. "You need not be afraid", the mystery person said in an effort to calm Ricabar down.

"I know you", Ricabar blurted out while panting with fright. "But it can't be you".

"Ahh, guess you recognize me now".

"Of course, I do. I've been dreaming of that face every night for the last eight years. But, but— " Ricabar stammered as he tried to comprehend what was happening.

"I know you have. In fact, I've made sure this face has been part of every thought you've had since you know when. How else could I get you to think about what you did"?

"But there's no way you can have that same face", Ricabar exclaimed.

The figure simply replied, "Way".

"But, but-," is all Ricabar could muster.

"But you think I cannot be him because of what you did", the cell guest said in finishing his statement.

Ricabar thought for a moment as he silently stared at the person before his eyes. "Yes, you're right. It can't be you because I'm the one who iced you".

"Very good", the guest said. "I'm flattered that you recognize me now".

"Yes, but since I killed you, how can you be here at this moment. Am I dreaming?"

The guest smiled and then slapped Ricabar across the face before he could move away to avoid the fast-moving hand. "Did you feel that?"

"You're damn right I did. It hurt!" Ricabar shouted as he instinctively jumped into fighting position but thought better of it. He stood there with a frown on his face and then rubbed his hand over his painful face.

"Then you tell me if you're dreaming," the guest said with a wry smile.

Ricabar thought about the nightmares he had been experiencing and he realized not once during those episodes had he felt anything like he had just gone through. This was definitely different and very realistic. Though convinced that he was not likely dreaming, Ricabar still had trouble trying to figure out what was going on. "Alright. I may not be dreaming but if you're the guy I iced, how can you now be here? If you're not the guy I iced and only look like him, who are you and how do you know my name? What's happening here?"

"Tsk, tsk, Ricabar, Ricabar. So many questions. Let's see, for months now you have been pleading for me to make a personal visit to your cell. Now that I'm here you offend me by refusing to recognize who I am. Were you just yanking my chain?" he asked feigning offense.

"Wait! How do you know that? I mean, I wasn't yanking anyone's chain! No! No! But, how is that possible? This shit can't happen. I'm in a fucking solid steel and concrete cell".

"Ricabar. Shame on you. Do you really feel you need to use that kind of language in my presence?"

An embarrassed Ricabar quickly apologized. "Sorry, but I just don't understand how this can really happen. I mean, you look like a Mexican and not like, ah, like, well like him" he said as he pointed his finger upward.

"Oh, so you've seen him?" the figure said while pointing his finger upward as if to mock Ricabar.

Ricabar thought for a moment. "No, but I have a pretty good idea what he looks like".

"Oh. I see. So, what does he look like? Do you have an image in your head based on an account given by someone who claims to have seen me, or him?"

"Yeah. Well, no I haven't. I guess it's based on the images I've seen in the books I've read".

"And in your books did he look like this?" The figure asked as he morphed into the face of an old light skinned man with long white hair, wrinkled skin and a flowing white beard. "Or does he look like this?" He asked as he changed into a dark complected man with a black pompadour and thin mustache. "Or maybe this is what you think I should look like" he said as he changed once again into a female face with a blonde bouffant hairstyle.

"Oh, hell no. I mean, I don't think that is what he looks like, but…", Ricabar replied as his voice trailed off.

"If you've done as much reading as you tell me you have, then you should know I can look like anything I choose. Don't you agree?"

Ricabar scratched his head and pondered. "I suppose you're right, but I still don't get it. How is this possible?".

"I see you still have your doubts. I thought with all that reading you have done in here you would have developed some faith in me and not question what I do and how I do it. Perhaps this will convince you". The Guest then darkened one of the walls of the cell. Immediately the wall became a movie screen, and something began to show.

"What is that?" Ricabar asked.

"Hang on, son. Be patient. Focus on what you see on the screen,"

Ricabar reluctantly complied.

The scene playing on the wall showed a young but tall boy walking into an electronics store. The boy walked around through all the aisles and appeared to be looking for something. He then glanced towards the cashier station and noticed the person behind the counter was busy talking to another person. The boy then grabbed something from one of the shelves and slipped it into his pants. He walked slowly around another aisle before making his way to the door. When he exited the store, he walked a few steps away from the door and stopped as if he was waiting for someone. Then suddenly a police officer walked up to him and told the boy to remove what he had inside his pants. The boy raised both hands seemingly to indicate he had nothing, but the officer tapped his hand against the pants. The boy then grudgingly slipped his hand inside his pants and pulled out the item he had hidden there. He handed the item to the policeman who then gave it to the store employee who had just walked out to meet him. The officer then placed handcuffs on the boy and walked him over to the squad car.

"You recognize the boy in that scene?" the Guest asked.

Ricabar did not immediately respond as he was still gazing at the wall.

"Surely your big brain does not need that much time to process what you just saw", the Guest said teasingly.

"I know who that is!" Ricabar shouted. "Where'd you get that video? Was there a camera at the store at that time? I don't remember anyone saying there had been video of that!"

"No, Ricabar. There was no camera then. The scene is part of my personal collection. I have gazillions of scenes like these recorded in my library".

"Ahh, your shitting me man. How could anyone have a recording of me heisting a CD player if there was no camera?"

"Yes, who would be the one person capable of something like that?" the Guest asked facetiously.

"Damn, I must be dreaming," Ricabar said exasperatingly.

"You want me to slap you again?"

Ricabar quickly raised his hands to his face. "No. That's not necessary,"

"Ok, then. Take a look at this one," the Guest said as a new scene began playing on the wall. In it, a female looking older than her years was sitting on the floor of a barely lit room. She is seen taking a rubber cord and wrapping it around her arm right above the elbow. One end of the cord was gripped by her teeth and the other she held in her free hand as she tied it around the arm. She then took a needle and pierced her arm just as she released the rubber cord. After dispensing what was in the needle, she pulled the needle from her arm and dropped it on the floor. Then she laid her head back against the wall and closed her eyes as her body began slight spasmodic jerks. As the scene expanded on the wall, a young boy stood a few feet from the woman staring at her. The boy said nothing, but tears flowed from his eyes.

"Ahh, fu…! Ricabar began to exclaim but caught himself before finishing his expletive. "That's me in the video! I remember that! How'd you get video of that?" Before he could get an answer, Ricabar recalled his Guest's earlier explanation. "Oh, that's right. This is part of your collection, isn't it?" Tears began to flow from Ricabar's eyes as he remembered seeing his mother many times doing what was shown in the video. The Guest remained silent waiting for Ricabar to say something. Ricabar remained staring at the wall with a stunned look on his face even though the video was no longer playing, and the wall was blank. After a long pause, Ricabar regained his composure and finally conceded. "There is only one person who could do that."

"And who do you think that person could be?"

Ricabar moved closer to the figure and tried to look into his eyes. "Are you really God?"

The Guest smiled. "The one and only."

"But why do you look like, like, well, like him?"

The guest laughed softly and shook his head. "Ricabar, my son, I look and talk like the man whose life you took for a reason—".

"And that is—?" Ricabar quickly interrupted. Then catching himself, he backed off. "Sorry!"

A smile ran across the guest's face as he said, "If I came as a stranger, I would encounter more difficulties in convincing you of my real identity but if I appeared as someone whom you know is no longer on this earth, I'd have a good shortcut to your memory. Besides, I thought it was rather clever on my part, don't you agree?"

Ricabar stared at him with a skeptical look. "If you wanna know what I really think, I think it's kinda sneaky, but I guess I can understand your motive. Ahh, I mean assuming you are him?"

"Ricabar, do you still doubt me? I'm disappointed. I came here to answer your prayer and now you insult me by refusing to acknowledge me".

"No, no, it's not that. It's just that—", Ricabar paused when he couldn't explain. He saw the exasperation in his Guest's eyes, so he quickly changed his attitude. "I guess you're right. I am not fully convinced, and I can't say why. I mean, I want to believe you but I'm afraid."

"You're afraid of dying and since you never really expected me to answer your pleas, you want to stall your demise. You didn't think I would respond to you, did you?"

Ricabar hesitated for a moment but then acknowledged the accuracy of his guest's observation. "I suppose you're right. I mean, I kept praying that he would, or maybe I should say, you would, but I never imagined that it could actually happen. How could I know? This is really freaking me out!"

"Well, let me ask you this. Have you told anyone of your desire to have your soul removed from your physical existence?"

"No," Ricabar replied.

"Have you told anyone about your ideas of how to end the lives of all the inmates in prisons across the world, including yourself?"

"No, not at all. They would think I'm nuts".

"It's a rhetorical question, Ricabar, 'cause I already know the answer. So, if you've never told anyone of your deepest and most personal thoughts, how do you suppose I know about them?"

Ricabar pondered for a few seconds but hesitated in answering.

"That's a question I do want an answer from you," the guest said as he noticed the hesitation on Ricabar's part.

"Well, there's only one person I have told that to and that would be to my Lord in my prayers".

The guest took a bow and uttered, "Thank you. So then here I am. In the flesh, so to speak".

Ricabar stood silently still trying to make sense of what he was experiencing.

"You still have your doubts, huh?" the Guest questioned.

"No. It's not 'cause I have a doubt but I would like to ask you for something".

"What is that?"

"Since you have the ability to show videos of scenes from the past, would you be able to show me a video clip of my dad?"

The guest placed his hand on his chin. "Hmm, I don't know if that is a great idea. Not that I cannot do that, mind you. I just don't think you could handle that right now".

"Please! I don't even know what he looks like or where he could be. I could never find him on my own. This is the only way I can learn something about him. Couldn't you please grant me this small wish?"

"Well, I hesitate because I know it will hurt you seeing him after not knowing him all this time".

"I can handle it. Don't worry about me".

"Muy bien, but you were warned".

At that moment, a scene began to show on the wall. It slowly revealed a slender black man with glasses sitting at a desk. He had a pen in one hand and was signing several documents and then placing them to one side of the desk. Above his desk were large paintings of black men in fancy clothes and ornate sashes across their chests. The man would glance at the paintings periodically. Suddenly, a boy of about 10 years of age runs toward him, shouting, "papa". The man quickly embraced the boy and placed a kiss on his forehead.

"How are you, Jamile?" the man asks the boy.

"I'm great, papa. Are you ready to go home with me?" the child asks.

"No, Jamile. I cannot go just now. I have much work to do. The president is counting on me to get this work to him by tonight".

"But my soccer game is in one hour, papa. You're not going to miss it, are you?"

The man hugged the boy again and said, "if I finish this work quickly I will make your game, but you are going to have to let me get back to work now".

"You promise, papa?"

Before the man could answer a voice of a woman is heard saying, "Come now, Jamile. We must allow your father to do his work. Let's be going now".

"You go on, Jamile", the father said as the boy walked away from view and the wall went black.

Ricabar remained focused on the wall even though it was now blank. A tear ran down his cheek. He wiped it off as he turned to the Guest and asked, "Was that really my father?"

"Yes. That was Ricardo Barron Duvries."

"When did that take place?"

With a sympathetic look on his face, the Guest replied, "last year about this time".

"So, I have a brother?" he asked excitedly.

"Yes, you do. A sister as well, two years younger.

"Do they know anything about me?"

The guest sighed and hesitated for a moment. "Your father has never revealed your existence to them. They know nothing about their father's life in this country. I'm sorry".

Ricabar stood silently staring at the floor and took some time before he could try to utter a word. He opened his mouth, but nothing came out. Instead he shook his head from side to side.

"You still have your doubts, Ricabar?"

Ricabar stared at him and then sighed while a tear ran down his cheek. "I'm sorry. It's not that I have any doubt now, it's just that at this moment I have conflicting feelings about you being here".

"Explain to me your conflict. Maybe I can help you resolve it."

Ricabar smiled and began to explain. "In all the times I spent praying that you would cause my life to be taken since I knew very well that I was deserving of your punishment, I never realized that in asking for relief, you would actually appear before me in the body of a person I can plainly see and talk to. Now that you're here, I feel unworthy of being in your presence. I have done some terrible things in my life, so I don't feel worthy to stand here and see you live. At the same time, I feel a great sense of relief that justice will finally be imposed and that the true measure of justice means giving up my life for the one I took even though it will not bring him back to his family. You were right when you earlier said I was afraid of dying but that's not the entirety of my fear. I was afraid of dying before I could truly atone for my sin".

"Well said, Ricabar. I see you've been using all those brain cells I gave you, but I have not yet decided that taking your life is the measure of justice warranted in this case. The agony and frustration of being locked up with a death sentence hanging over your head and the uncertainty of when that sentence will ever be carried out seems like a pretty good punishment to me so far. I came here to allow you to try to convince me that the sentence you want me to impose on you is truly what I should do for you".

A startled and confused Ricabar bent over to look into the eyes of the smaller figure and said, "I just presumed that you were here to grant my wish by taking my life. I'm really ready to die. I don't understand."

"I know and perhaps that is what I will command but—"

"Oh, I'm sorry" Ricabar interrupted. "I shouldn't have been so presumptive".

"No, it's okay. I'm not going to hold that against you. Why don't we talk about why you prayed for the relief you so much want to receive"?

"You want to take time to talk to me?"

"Of course! You do not want me to just wave my hand and make it all happen, do you? What's the fun in that?"

"I find this all very confusing, but I appreciate you wanting to talk to me."

"Think nothing of it. I do this quite frequently. Besides, I have plenty of time and no other place I need to be right now."

"Well, okay", Ricabar said as he looked around for a place for his Guest to sit. "Can we sit down? I'm afraid I have no chair to offer you. Perhaps we can both sit on my bed."

"That's quite hospitable of you but that won't be necessary. I'll just take this and sit down," the Guest replied as he pulled a small wooden bench out of thin air and accommodated it right next to the bed and motioned to Ricabar to sit. He then pulled a chair again from thin air and straddled it, his body facing the back of the chair quite casually as he faced Ricabar.

If there was any doubt left in his mind about the identity of his Guest, this gesture removed it. "What do you want me to talk about?" Ricabar sheepishly asked.

The Guest smiled and replied, "why don't you tell me about the time when you took my life?"

"Your life?" a surprised Ricabar asked. "I didn't take your life, did I? I mean—"

"Well, not my life per se, but you did ice one of my children so in essence, you iced me".

"Geez, I suppose you are correct," Ricabar acquiesced. "But I thought you knew all about what I did so why do I have to tell you?"

"Ah, yes, it has been said that I am all knowing, but I still want to hear all the details from your lips. It's part of you making your case to me, you see," he said peering into Ricabar's eyes. "You're not afraid to tell me, are you?"

"Oh no! It's not that... well, I see, but…," he replied as he struggled to collect his thoughts in preparation for giving the factual narrative of his case. He looked at the ceiling while the moments of the night when he committed the ultimate crime flashed before his mind's eye. Ricabar knew he had to get every detail right as he could not fool or mislead his Guest. It had been years since he had given more than a passing thought to his crime, so he had not revisited the disheartening details and his labored breathing made it obvious that he was not pleased with the re-creation of the images in his mind. The Guest stared patiently at him.

After spending several minutes pondering about what to say, he finally gathered his thoughts and began his explanation.

"I knew I shouldn't have left the house that night. Something told me there would be trouble bigger than I could handle but I kept hearing the pleas from my mother. She needed her fix and she had nothing. I remember her begging me to go out and get her some cat's pee and I kept telling her 'no' 'cause I wanted her to go cold turkey but she kept on screaming that she was in pain and desperately needed her bubble gum. I was tired of being the one who fed her habit, but I couldn't stand hearing her cry, so, I went out and got my buddy Chifon and we went looking for a chinkmart we could hit. We thought if we went over to the west side we might find one we hadn't hit before so after driving around, Chifon pointed to one that was still open that late at night. We must have been too cocky or too stupid but neither one of us put anything on to hide our faces. I wasn't too concern 'cause it was Chifon who had the gun but he was never gonna pull the trigger when it came down to it. He was too scared of guns and besides, it wasn't loaded. He just used it to scare people. We both went inside and Chifon walked up to the clerk and pointed the gun right at his face and told him to give us the money. As I was standing behind Chifon, someone grabbed my arm and said, 'you guys shouldn't be doing this.' I turned around and saw, ah, well, you or the guy you look like. He was still holding my arm when Chifon turned around and pointed the gun right at the store clerk, but he didn't seem to be scared. All I could think to do was to grab the Mexican dude by the neck. I lifted him up and kept squeezing harder as I told Chifon to get out. When I saw him run out the door I turned around and threw the little Mexican dude down to the floor and started to walk toward the door. That's when I heard a loud bang and felt something hit me on my back side and I fell down. I put my hand on my butt where I felt the pain and I realized I was bleeding. The chink had shot me in the ass with a shotgun. I couldn't believe the pain, but I tried to get up to walk to the door. I saw Chifon drive away just as I hit the floor and then I lost consciousness. Next thing I remember I woke up in a hospital chained to a bed with a cop standing next to me. When I asked him what had happened, he said I had killed a young Hispanic male by the name of Julio Estelar at the store I was trying to rob. I said nothing, but I began to remember what had happened that night. Two days later I was in the Bexar County jail facing capital murder charges. A year later I was convicted and sentenced to death and I've been here ever since as you already know."

"Very interesting. I don't need to tell you that was a terrible thing you did that night but I'm curious about one thing."

"I know, and I have been agonizing about it ever since. The overwhelming sense of guilt has been eating at me every night."

"Well, we'll deal with that part later but now I want to talk about something else."

"What is that? I didn't leave anything out" Ricabar stated defensively.

The Guest raised his hand to signal Ricabar to stop. "Why did you feel that you had to take my life to get what you wanted that night?"

"But it wasn't you that I iced," Ricabar protested. "I know you look like him and talk like him, but it wasn't you that night."

"You find that uncomfortable, don't you? That I look and talk like the man you killed with your bare hands. Why is that?"

"I don't want to accept that it was you I killed that night! It wasn't you!"

The Guest said nothing but stared directly at Ricabar much like a parent would stare at a child refusing to acknowledge the truth.

Seeing the Guest staring at him, Ricabar bowed his head and softly uttered, "I know it's a part of the lesson you're trying to teach me, but it augments the emotional torment I'm already suffering, and it shames me to no end."

"I see. At least my method is proving effective, but let's get back to my question."

Ricabar looked up at his Guest and thought for a while about how best to answer. "I didn't want a witness to finger me and Chifon," was his explanation.

His Guest shook his head and said, "But you weren't planning on killing the store clerk and he would have been a witness. I don't think you're being honest with yourself and I know you're not telling me the whole truth."

"Well, if you already know, why are you asking me?" Ricabar asked belligerently.

The Guest stared right at Ricabar as he shook his head and said," Ricabar, before you can receive your just punishment and be forgiven, you must understand and acknowledge, not only what you did, but why you did it."

"But I accept my guilt. Isn't it enough that I admit that I took the life of Julio Estelar while trying to rob a store at gunpoint. I admit I'm guilty of what I was convicted. What else do I need to do to get my just punishment? I can't take being in this place anymore!" an exasperated Ricabar exclaimed.

The Guest smiled in an effort to hide his frustration with his host and said, "Perhaps if we took a closer look at the events of that night you might realize what I'm talking about." He then turned to the wall opposite the bed and pointed to it with his raised hand. Immediately another scene began playing like a movie in front of them. "Do you recognize this scene you're watching?"

"Yes," a surprised Ricabar replied as he stood up to get a closer look. "Is that from the store's video camera or is this another one from your collection?"

"No, of course not. If it were from the store, you would have seen it during your trial. No. As I told you, I have the greatest collection of videos you will ever see. I can replay every scene of every person's life since man first walked on this earth, but let's not digress. Do you see yourself in the video?"

Ricabar looked stunned by the explanation but acknowledged his role in the video. "Yes, I see myself and Chifon entering the store."

"Well, play close attention to the scene when Julio walks in and catches you two in the act."

Ricabar paid close attention as he saw Julio walk in and approach him while Chifon held the gun to the clerk's face.

As Julio approaches Ricabar, the video shows him grabbing Ricabar's left buttock and squeezing it. The audio reveals Julio's rather effeminate voice telling him that he shouldn't be doing that and then he looks straight up at Ricabar with a smile on his face. Ricabar slaps at Julio's hand and in a fit of anger grabs the diminutive Julio by the neck and lifts him up while yelling, "You fuckin faggot," as he shakes him like a rag doll.

Upon seeing this, Ricabar turns away and yells, "Stop it! Please stop. I don't need to see any more."

He fell back to the bed and the stunned look on his face revealed to his Guest that the point was received.

The Guest stopped the video, turned to Ricabar and asked, "What answer would you now like to give to my question?"

Ricabar spent a long moment in silence agonizing over his thoughts before responding.

"You mean, why did I kill him?"

The Guest nodded and replied, "Precisely."

"In my defense," Ricabar began as he paused to make sure he stated his position clearly, "I must have suppressed that aspect of the events that night for whatever reason. I did not mean to deliberately mislead you about what I did that night and why. I just didn't remember that detail."

"I know, but now do you understand why I posed my question to you?" The Guest asked as he pulled his chair over closer to the bed and sat down. He then mysteriously raised his hand to his lips as it was now holding a wine glass with a red liquid in it. He could tell by the expression on Ricabar's face that he was wondering what he had in his hand. Without waiting for a question, he explained, "2001 Corison Kronos Cabernet. One of the best cabs around. Some of my children have really learned to make a really fine wine. Would you like some?" He offered while enjoying a sip.

Ricabar shook his head and replied, "I don't drink, thanks."

The Guest smiled at him and repeated his question. "Explain to me why you chose to break Julio's neck. It can't be because he posed a physical threat to you, is it? No, of course, not. He was five foot 4, as you can see," he said as he pointed to himself. "And you at six foot six, weighing almost three times as me, just not a fair fight. Don't you agree?"

"No, I wasn't afraid he was going to hurt me. That wasn't it," Ricabar responded while lowering his head now feeling greatly embarrassed by his admission.

"No, I gathered as much. So, tell me what was it that made you feel compelled to take his life?"

Ricabar raised his head to face his interrogator, prepared to give the true answer. "He made a pass at me and insulted my masculinity 'cause I'm not gay," he argued in an angry tone. "He should have never done that. Guys like him deserve what they get."

The Guest leaned back and with disappointment in his voice asked, "So, that justified the drastic action you took?"

"Yes," Ricabar replied without thinking but quickly realized that was not the right response. "Well, no, I can't say that I was justified in killing him because of that but those people have no business being around. You yourself have said so."

"Whoa, wait a minute. Give that to me again."

"I rid this earth of someone who didn't deserve to live amongst us."

"Hang on a second, Ricabar Dane! I am incredulous. You want to justify your crime by claiming it is something I desire? You think you're justified in getting rid of one of those guys," using air quotes, "because I condone such actions?"

"Well, you said it in the Bible, didn't you? Doesn't the Bible say it is a sin to be gay. They're a perversion and not God-like and they deserve to be killed. Isn't that what you said in Leviticus 20:13?"

The Guest shook his head from side to side. "Let's get something straight here, Ricabar. You may have read something along those lines but let me clarify it for you. I did not write the Bible. Not one single word. To be even more clear, I have never said to anyone that gays are immoral or un-Me-like, much less that they deserve to be killed."

"What do you mean you didn't write the Bible?" Ricabar asked in disbelief. That's not what we've been told by every preacher, priest, or clergy person who ever took the pulpit. Weren't they quoting you when they've said that? Why would they want us to believe that if that's not what you said?"

While exercising restraint and being extremely patient and logical, the Guest replied, "I realize that, but don't you think I would know if I actually said or wrote something? Does the Bible say, 'Written by God' or have you seen my signature on it?"

"Another rhetorical question?", Ricabar asked with a sense of self-congratulation.

"Now you're getting it," the Guest said with a smile. "Look Ricabar. A collection of men and some women along the way produced that book but my hand did not pen any of the things you read in it. It is also claimed that the writers were inspired by me to write what they did and perhaps that may be true. After all, I am an inspirational kind of guy. Well, at least in their minds they may have felt inspiration from me, but as much as people of the cloth have tried to convince the masses that the Bible represents my word, I must plead 'not guilty' as I am not the author. Don't get me wrong, I think there are very clever and positive thoughts expressed in those writings and some are very good advice and worthy of attention. There's a lot I consider garbage too. But the point is, I cannot claim any credit for any of the content of that book."

"But I've also read in there that you gave the words to those who put it together and that it was written in your name."

"Yeah, well that's a self-serving statement, made to give the book credibility, especially to the gullible. But I can tell you that the persons who wrote it or portions of it, reflected in their writings what they perceived and assumed were my views and thoughts. However, along the way they included the biases and prejudices prevalent at the time. While they were, without a doubt, intelligent human beings, they lacked the sophistication possessed by many better-educated and rational people of your time. Unfortunately, homosexuality was deemed to be against my principles because those with the pen found it offensive to their mores. By mentioning it in their book, they gave it greater significance than it merited and created the impression that I frowned upon those who possessed such traits. Apparently, it worked as many now mistakenly are of the attitude that homosexuality does not meet with my approval."

"Are you telling me that is not the case?"

"That is exactly what I'm telling you. Let me ask you this. Do you believe that I created every living thing on Earth?'

"Yes, I do."

"Well, then do you really think that I would create a creature only so that it could be subjected to disdain and mistreatment done in my name, with my approval? And do you really think I would have my children killed simply because they laid down together? I realize I made those who prefer humans of the opposite sex but what harm have they suffered at the hands of those who prefer their kind? Do anything that homosexuals do in being who they are cause any harm to anyone else? So, they do not reproduce when they get together but there's plenty of offspring coming from heterosexuals in the world. Not a problem in my eyes."

"Are you telling me that a person who is gay or lesbian is that way because you made him or her like that? They are not choosing to be that way?"

"That is exactly what I am telling you. Did you choose to be black?"

"No. I had no say so in that."

"Did you choose to be as tall as you are?"

"Well, not how tall I am but I guess I did choose to be as heavy as I am by deciding what and how much to eat."

"Yes, you're right that one does come from the choices you made. But I see you get my point. There are characteristics of the person you are such as race, hair color, eye color that are innate. They are determined at the time of your birth. Most people understand this but what they fail to understand is that things such as sexual identity or preference are also traits that are equally innate. Sadly, some children of mine lived in the world long before they could figure this out. Instead, they formed a simplistic view of life and believed that certain things were considered normal. Anything that did not conform to their idea of what was normal was considered immoral or un-Me-like, but I did not establish for them what was or was not normal. I only created what is real and actually seen by everyone. Unfortunately, once they established what they considered normal and acceptable, their views were passed on to every succeeding generation. You believed that view, so I repeat my question, since you did not answer it when I asked it earlier. Do anything that homosexuals do in being who they are cause any harm to anyone else?"

Ricabar was taken aback by what sounded like a scolding from his Guest. He thought for a moment before answering. He then began shaking his head and said, "I admit I cannot think of any such harm, so the answer must be 'No.' I see your point."

'Let me give you another example. You've read in the bible that slavery is acceptable and because of that many in the world at one time considered it their right to own and dominate other human beings as slaves. In fact, a whole section of your country fought to the death to preserve what they erroneously believed to be their God-given right to own your ancestors as slaves. It took thousands of years for man to realize and accept that slavery is wrong, yet some still cling to the opposing belief simply because it is sanctioned in the Bible. Now do you honestly believe that I created human beings so that they could be subjugated by their brethren?"

Ricabar stared at him and then hesitatingly asked, "That is a rhetorical question, right? I mean, you certainly do not expect me to reply affirmatively to that?"

"You catch on quickly Ricabar. I would think that you would have no difficulty in seeing the vagarious shortcomings of slavery. Am I right?"

"Yes, of course, Lord! I can certainly tell you that I find no virtue in the practice and how it survived until the 19th century is frightening and disturbing to me."

"Well, I can tell you that if some people in this day and time had their way, slavery would be reinstated. But let's get back to the point I was making. Throughout history, man has sought to legitimize unsavory practices by seeking refuge in the Bible while proclaiming that certain proscriptions of conduct he finds offensive were commanded by me simply by including them in this book. Don't you think that's rather presumptive of man to speak for me by declaring in his Bible that it is I who has dictated that such conduct be prohibited?" The Guest looked at Ricabar as if to wait for a response.

Ricabar saw him staring and quickly said, "Oh, I thought that was another rhetorical question, but you're right. It is quite presumptive of man to think that? But in that vein, I was under the impression that, though you may not have written the Bible, you directed those who did by delivering messages to them by some medium or another. Am I to think that my impression is misplaced?"

"Ricabar, I will not tell you that I never make direct contact with my children for then how would you believe that I am here before you, but my message to those with whom I have spoken throughout history is not going to contradict my fundamental principle. For example, in Leviticus 20:18, the Bible dictates that any man who has sex with a woman who is in her menstruation cycle shall be exiled and isolated from his people along with the woman. Are you serious? You're really going to condemn a man and a woman for doing such a thing in the privacy of their own home?"

"Now I know that's a rhetorical question but if you will permit me to speculate, I would say that at some point in time, and a long time ago at that, someone complained about the act of intercourse with a woman in her period for whatever reason, and maybe it was an influential woman herself who complained, and those in authority declared that to be unlawful. Then it evolved into a more serious 'crime,'" Ricabar said while making air quotation marks with his fingers, "such that someone suggested that the act be included in the Bible as conduct to be declared as unholy or frowned upon by you and that's why we see it in the book today. Am I right?" he asked with a certain pride in himself.

"The Guest smiled and replied, "You strike me as a rather perceptive fellow, Ricabar. It's a shame you wasted the talent I gave you. But I digress. I don't quite understand why man thinks that I am such a micromanager that I would provide a rule for such trivial matters. Kind of insults my intelligence, don't you think?"

"If that last part was not a rhetorical question I would say, 'indeed.' But more directly to your point, Lord. I am sorry I did not utilize the gifts you gave me. That shames me to no end, especially since I've been in this cell, but you're making me try too hard to focus on your questions to determine which are rhetorical and which are not. That's giving me a headache."

"Don't be such a weenie, Ricabar," he said as he laughed and sipped on his wine.

Ricabar laughed as he appreciated his Guest's sense of humor. "Okay, Lord, I give you that one."

"I also can't understand why man thinks he needs to complicate matters. It's really very simple, Ricabar. If everyone followed its simplicity, man wouldn't need any laws. And God knows I hate laws, or rather, I know I hate laws. That's a little God humor, Ricabar. Can you dig it? But I digress again. Anyway, laws tell me that man isn't following my fundamental principle and too many are behaving badly such that others feel a law must be pronounced to outlaw such behavior."

Ricabar stared at his Guest intensely with a quizzical look on his face. His Guest noticed and stated, "What? Why are you giving me that look?"

Ricabar smiled as the accent in his voice and the mannerisms of the Julio whose image he had assumed came through. "You've been referring to it as if I was already aware of it. Don't you think you should tell me what your fundamental principle is, so I can understand what you're talking about?"

The Guest smiled and nodded in agreement. "I suppose you do deserve that bit of information. You know Ricabar, it's really very simple. I created every one of you with the right to be free to do or be anything you want as long as in doing so, you do not adversely affect someone else's right to do or be what he or she wants. That is my fundamental principle. Ideally, if every single person on earth followed this principle in every aspect of his or her life, you wouldn't need any laws and peace would dominate the world."

"That's it? That's the fundamental principle?"

"Yes. I told you it was very simple. As I said to you, things need not be complicated to be effective."

"Well, if anyone knows that Earth is not the ideal world it's you, Lord," Ricabar brazenly pointed out before realizing he was being unusually forward and then backed off. "I mean, if it is a simple concept, I don't get why man has not recognized it and followed it".

"Well, as I said, man unnecessarily complicates things. Many of the things man finds unacceptable and thus outlaws do not actually violate the fundamental principle. Can you give me examples of such laws, Ricabar?"

"Is this an exam, Lord?"

"Oh, come on, Ricabar. Humor me. You've read many things while in here. What laws do you find do not violate the fundamental principle?"

Ricabar thought for a while before answering. "I suppose that the laws criminalizing homosexual conduct would be one example. I can't think of anyone's fundamental right being adversely affected by someone practicing such conduct. Am I right?"

"That's right. There have been gay and lesbian people on Earth since the beginning of time. Not once in that time has any person's fundamental right been abridged or violated by any homosexual person being what and who they are."

"What about when a gay man sexually abuses a male child? Would that be deemed a violation of the child's fundamental right?"

"That would be a violation because there is a physical assault committed against the child who has a right not to be assaulted but that is totally different than the man being gay. It is not the fact that the man is gay that is causing the abridgement of the child's right…"

"It is the physical assault," Ricabar injected.

"Precisely. What do you think are other examples?"

"Laws that prohibited my kind to drink out of public water fountains or sit with white people on buses. I don't see what right of whites I would violate if I quenched my thirst with a water fountain used by them. We all need water. I have the same germs they have. Just because I'm black doesn't mean a white person who drinks after me is going to be physically harmed."

The Guest shook his head up and down in agreement but said nothing.

"You're not talking about just this country, are you?" Ricabar asked.

"Not at all but you are right. Even though I created humans with differences, such as race, skin color and other physical traits, I did not make one superior over the other. Differences were meant to provide the Earth with variety as I am not fond of boring things. When one race thinks it is superior over others, it begins to do many things which end up violating my fundamental principle. This is common in other parts of the world, not just your country."

"That makes sense to me, Lord. I can see how differences in human beings should be used to benefit all instead of creating conflict."

"Very good, Ricabar. What else can you see?"

"Well, then I can see that laws prohibiting women in certain countries from doing many things or limiting what they can wear in public don't seem to prevent violations of anyone's fundamental right. If they want to wear a dress like women in this country, what violation of someone else's fundamental right would they be guilty of? I mean, I can't see why countries can justify forcing women to cover themselves up because men could get tempted if the women revealed parts of their bodies. Why can't men just learn to control themselves? And why can't women be allowed to drive in some countries? Boy don't get me started!"

"You're on to something, Ricabar. Those are good examples but give me something far more substantial."

Ricabar had to think long and hard and then came up with what he thought fit the bill. "You may not see this my way, Lord, but I think laws prohibiting prostitution are contrary to the fundamental principle."

"How so?"

"What a woman does with her body with anyone doesn't violate anyone else's fundamental right. If she is willing to accept money from someone who is willing to pay her money for having sex, who's fundamental right is being adversely affected? I'll answer my own question. Nobody. That's who. In fact, I would say such laws violate her fundamental right to be or do what she wants."

"I'm puzzled by your selection. Does it hit something close to you?"

"Nothing gets past you, Lord. Yes, I say this in defense of my mother 'cause I recognize what she was going through. She was only hurting herself by doing what she was doing. She didn't deserve to be jailed for that!"

"You don't see any merit to such laws?"

"No. I don't. Sorry Lord."

"No need to be sorry, Ricabar."

"I do understand that these are morality laws. I mean, they are in the books because somebody felt this type of behavior by a woman is considered 'immoral' but what is immoral to one is not necessarily immoral to another. Who decides what is or is not immoral?"

"I have to admit you have a valid point, Ricabar. To carry out the fundamental principle I gave everyone free will. It is essential to allow a person to decide what to be or do. For example, I created and made sexual intercourse between two consenting adults enjoyable for several reasons. To promote the procreation of humans is the most important one. It is also a means for expressing intimacy between two individuals who care for and love each other. However, a woman, or man for that matter, who is willing to engage in sexual conduct with another willing participant in exchange for money is an exercise in free will and I have to admit does not violate anyone else's fundamental right."

"I may seem to be contradicting myself but what if the one paying money contracts a transmittable disease? Would the one getting paid be considered violating the payer's fundamental right?"

"It is the same for both. If there is voluntariness on both parts, wouldn't they each know there are risks in engaging in such conduct? And wouldn't their carrying out the agreed transaction not be an indication that each is willing to accept such risks?"

"Forgive me for saying, Lord, but aren't you sounding like a lawyer?" Ricabar said in an attempt to lighten up the discussion.

The Guest smiled. "Whatever gets you to understand the points Ricabar. Are you with me?"

"Absolutely, Lord."

"Then we are in agreement. A person can engage in sexual conduct for money without violating anyone else's fundamental right. I think you get what I'm telling you about the simplicity of my concept."

"I can see the beauty of the concept, but I can also see that many of us do not adhere to it. Like me, for instance, the way I understand your principle, I now see how I violated it by depriving Julio of his right to be. That is, by breaking his neck I deprived him of his right to live. I can't think of a more serious violation of your principle than that. Am I right?"

The comment and question brought a smile to his Guest. "I see that you have a keen appreciation of my concept, so now you can explain to me why you chose to violate it."

Ricabar paused for a moment and then began, "As far as the store clerk is concerned, I interfered with his right to be free from being robbed of his money because I needed to get my mother her fix. Poor excuse, I know, but that was my motivation. The clerk did get a measure of revenge by shooting me in the ass, as you saw in the video." He took a deep breath, as he was aware that his Guest wanted an explanation for taking Julio's life. "At that moment, I felt an ire so intense when he made that pass at me that I instinctively retaliated by grabbing his neck. The more I felt that he thought I was his kind the harder I squeezed my hand around his neck. Did I feel threatened by him? No. I just felt insulted and dissed by his sexually suggestive gesture."

"Are you that insecure about your own masculinity that you would allow such an innocuous gesture to define whether you are gay or not? More importantly, was your extreme reaction necessary to dispel any notion that you welcomed the gesture?"

Ricabar realized he had been placed in a tough spot with these questions. What had been a moment of levity now had gotten serious and solemn. He scratched his head and rubbed his brow with his hand and then took a deep breath. "I guess if you put it that way, I have to admit I grossly overreacted and looking back at that moment, I realize I thought then that if I had done nothing in response to his physical advances it would have been an indication that I shared in his homosexuality. I see now that's not the case. Oh my God, I killed him for nothing and that makes my crime even worse than I thought," he cried out as he began to tear up. He shook his head from side to side and then continued while sobbing, "I am so sorry Julio! I admit that I deprived you of your fundamental right and there's nothing that could ever justify that. For that I am very sorry Lord!" he offered while falling to his knees. His sobs grew louder. He hugged the legs of his Guest and suddenly realized he could actually feel them as he hugged them tightly. If there were any remnant doubts in his mind he was not dreaming, they were quickly dispelled.

The Guest stood up from his chair and placed his hand on Ricabar's head, which was bowed, but before he could say anything, Ricabar continued. "I know what I did is unforgiveable and even if it isn't, I feel no merit in any request for forgiveness. That is why I have been pleading to you that I be met with the only punishment that is warranted and that is, that you swiftly do away with me without further deliberation."

The Guest motioned to Ricabar to get up and sit on the bed while he sat back on his bench. "Your sincerity pleases me, Ricabar, but do you believe that the death penalty is a just punishment for what you did?"

"It makes all the sense to me, Lord. The way I see it, if I committed the ultimate invasion of someone's fundamental right by taking his life, then I must pay by forfeiting mine. Is that not justice in your eyes?"

"Your words are impressive as I see you have enlightened yourself. But let's talk about the punishment you seek from me. Before I can consider your request, I need something from you first and you touched upon it a second ago."

Ricabar stared at the Guest and wondered what that could be. He instinctively replied, "I said I was sorry, didn't I?"

"Yes, but you presumed that you could not be forgiven by me for committing such an unspeakable crime."

"But I also recognized that my deed is unforgiveable. Isn't that true?"

"My dear Ricabar, did you not read in your book that I am known as the forgiving father? That part is true, but forgiveness comes to those who seek atonement. We have a saying in our Mexican culture that goes, 'El que no habla, ni Dios lo oye', which means, 'he who does not speak, cannot be heard even by me.' "Another bit of God humor."

Ricabar smiled. "I see. So, you're saying that if I ask for forgiveness, I will receive it?"

"If you are sincere in your plea and truly regret your crime, that is what you will get. You cannot be welcomed in my home upon leaving your earth unless you receive my forgiveness but that has to be in response to your sincere desire to be forgiven."

Ricabar again dropped to his knees and while reaching out to touch his Guest's hand, said, "Lord, I am truly sorry for having taken Julio's life and I beg your forgiveness."

The Guest extended his hand and placed upon Ricabar's head and said, "Stand up Ricabar as I forgive you for taking my child's life."

Ricabar smiled at the Guest as he felt an eerie warmth throughout his body. Gone was the unrelenting guilt that kept him awake all those nights. Instead, he felt a comforting calmness that caused any hint of a fear of death to disappear.

The Guest took a final sip from his wine glass which then suddenly disappeared and said, "Now, let's discuss the punishment you have been seeking. Tell me again. Why do you think I should carry out such a final act?"

"You mean 'final' but only as it concerns life on Earth, right?" Ricabar asked with nervousness in his voice.

"Very good, Ricabar. I see you've been paying attention. Yes, I mean why should your life on Earth come to an end?"

Ricabar smiled and replied, "Because I do not deserve to be among the living having committed such an egregious violation of your fundamental principle. My life should be taken in payment for the one I took, and I really believe that would be justice."

The Guest looked right into Ricabar's eyes and also heard his heart begin to race in the silence of the cell. After a brief moment, he smiled and declared, "Your sense of justice appeals to me Ricabar. You make a compelling case for the granting of your wish but tell me this. Do you think that all of those incarcerated in this place with you deserve a similar fate?"

"Without a doubt, Lord," Ricabar replied without hesitation. "Everyone one of us here violated your fundamental principle in the worst ways. So, yes, they all merit such a fate. And you can include all those incarcerated in every prison across this planet, save and except those who truly are innocent which I'm sure you can pick out. I think every person who has violated man's laws has demonstrated a total lack of respect for his fellow man and I see it as a declaration that they do not want to be a member of society. Therefore, they should be gone. However, as you have demonstrated with me, if any of those deserving of the ultimate punishment can ask and receive your forgiveness, and then they will find the solace in the new place just like me. Right?"

"Ok. That's interesting. And yes, you are right. Anyone who has violated the fundamental principle can be granted my forgiveness and they will join you in the 'new place', as you called it." The Guest paused for a moment as he rubbed his hand against his chin. He then asked, "Anyone else whom you believe should experience the deadly consequences of your deadly mist you have been proposing?"

"Well, Lord. I've thought long and hard about this one 'cause I know my mother considered doing it to me but I have a big problem with aborting a fetus. After all, if I understand science well enough, doesn't a human being begin when the male sperm has joined with a female ovum? I mean, everything evolves from that single event and leads to the birth of a new creature so that eliminating it at some point in between seems like a violation your fundamental principle. Doesn't it?"

"You make a good point Ricabar, but are you reacting out of resentment for your mother for thinking about doing that to you or does that reflect a true and honest position on your part?"

"Well, why don't you tell me if I'm wrong? I know the laws say that a woman has a right to control her own body but how can you reconcile that notion with the fact that a life begins when the woman physically joins with a man?"

"I'm not saying you are wrong, Ricabar. I certainly appreciate your ideas. After all, as I said earlier, I did make sexual intercourse fun and enjoyable for the purpose of encouraging reproduction of your kind. And that goes for every living creature. How else could you maintain your species and prevent yourselves from becoming extinct. If having sex were not pleasurable, who would want to engage in coitus and how could I keep the Earth populated?"

"Precisely, Lord! You get it. Right?"

The Guest looked at Ricabar somewhat incredulously and Ricabar quickly recognized that he was being rather presumptuous about giving his approval of his Guest's position. "Sorry, Lord. I know you don't need my approval and I certainly do not need to convince you of anything. I apologize."

"That's quite alright, Ricabar. However, that one seems to generate more questions than answers. For instance, would you punish a woman who was impregnated by someone with whom the woman did not consent to having intercourse, such as a rapist or an incester?"

"I see your point." Ricabar pondered for a moment and then said, "But the result of that wrong encounter is still a life, isn't it?"

"No question, Ricabar. So how would you handle the life that became of such encounter?"

"If the woman did not want to be tied to the product of that violation of the fundamental principle, she could always let someone else raise it to adulthood. I mean, if my mother did not want me, I would have been okay with her giving me away and let someone else raise me although if she had aborted me I would not have grown up to take Julio's life. Man, what a tough quandary I've created. What's the answer, Lord?"

"Yes, it is quite a quandary. And you are correct in that we have two conflicting interests. On the one hand we have a life, tiny as it is but nevertheless a life with its own fundamental right, and on the other, the mother's fundamental right to control her own body. The difference between the two is that the tiny life had no choice in its beginning. On the other side we have the mother, who in most instances, engaged in sexual intercourse knowing that a possible consequence of such action is to begin a new life. I chose to have the woman carry that new life as I had to choose between the man or the woman. Since I made the man stronger to protect the woman and the new life, I made the woman stronger to handle the growing of the new life in her until it can live on its own. I placed a huge burden upon her, I understand, but I also rewarded her with the joy of motherhood once she completed the process. I entrusted her with the life of another child of mine. In those instances when the man and woman come together voluntarily and create a new life, whether they intended that or not, to abort it would be a violation of the new life's fundamental right to continue its life until it could live on its own. This is so because every life, either at the beginning or at any point between then and death is conferred with the fundamental principle to be."

"What about when a man and a woman do not come together voluntarily, and a new life is created? You know, in a case of rape."

"In that instance, the new life would still be clothed with the fundamental principle and right to be. However, the man in that case would be deemed to have violated the woman's fundamental right to be free from such assault and should be made to suffer the consequences."

"So, abortion would be still be wrong in that instance, Lord?"

"Yes, of course. I cannot remove the new life's fundamental right even if created under the most egregious circumstances. I regret that my creation of the reproductive system is unable to distinguish between the circumstances of how the new life is created. That is a burden I have placed on human beings and all creatures on earth. But remember, a life once commenced does not cease to be a life at any stage, even when it is dependent on another before it can survive on its own."

"Essentially what I understand is that if you do not want to take the chance of creating a new life then do not have sexual intercourse or have it but use a method which prevents the coming together of a sperm and egg?"

"That is correct, Ricabar. Sometimes humans cannot have it all their way, so they are faced with difficult choices to make. Remember you all have free will. If you exercise that free will in a way which does not violate the fundamental principle I will be pleased."

"What if the mother's life is in danger and the only way to save her is to sacrifice the new life? Would that violate the fundamental principle?"

"It would, Ricabar. You see, the taking of any life is the one absolute violation of the fundamental principle. However, that quandary is not for man to resolve on Earth. Man was not given the right to create a law to foreclose the woman from making her choice. After all, I did not appoint man as my proxy on Earth. But, do not forget that even when humans violate the fundamental principle, I am still the forgiving God. I would consider all mitigating factors in deciding when to forgive someone wanting to join me in my kingdom, even when the violation is the ultimate deprivation of someone else's fundamental right, as you well know."

"I get it, Lord." Ricabar stated with an understanding tone. "Now I see that every life is sacred and it's not to be taken by any man or woman. However, what if someone takes a life when trying to protect another's life, including his own? Like the store clerk. If he had killed me while I was killing Julio, would he have violated the fundamental principle?"

"What did I just say, Ricabar?" The Guest asked as he glared at Ricabar.

"Oops. My bad. I see it now. Yes, he would but because he iced me to try to save Julio, he would be forgiven for violating the fundamental principle, assuming he asked for forgiveness."

The Guest placed each hand on the side of his head and while simultaneously and quickly moving the hands away from his head, said "boom!"

"Some more of your God humor, huh? Ricabar exclaimed with a smile.

"Yes, and all I will tell you is that every life is sacred. Even I do not find any comfort in seeing anyone's death. I know I get assigned with a lot of blame for many disasters but even though I created nature, I have to let it take its course and the result of that is many times unpleasant to see."

The Guest directed his gaze at Ricabar and with a sad face said, "Ricabar, I wish you had chosen a different path for yourself for I see in you a wise man even though you ducked an education. You could have done so well for yourself but for some bad choices. Your understanding of my explanations impresses me, but I will have to think long and hard before I include any woman who has chosen to end the life inside her in the mist you seek. Anyone else that merits the Ricabar fate?"

Ricabar pondered for a moment and then suggested, "You know what I've grown to really detest?"

"What is that?"

"It's a rhetorical question Lord."

"My bad. I knew that," the Guest said with a snicker.

Ricabar smiled and uttered, "Gotcha."

"Touché, Ricabar. Just don't get too cocky."

"Ok. As I was saying, I've really grown to detest hypocrisy and I can't stand hypocrites."

"What, you want me to eliminate all Republicans?" the Guest interrupted with a sly smile.

Ricabar began to laugh. "That's a good one Lord. But, I suppose that would be too harsh a penalty even though I find it completely disdainful. Maybe if you could just make them suffer an annoying illness for a while."

"I see. Anyone else you find deserving of such a fate?"

"I think anyone who commits an act of violence in your name should meet such a fate as well. You know, those who in your name and loyalty to their religion take a multitude of lives thinking that they will be rewarded in heaven. I also do not think a religion which has, as its main objective, to violate the fundamental principle of all within its control is worthy. How can such a religion justify its existence when it imposes antiquated and unjust laws?"

"I think I know to whom you are referring. I can tell you that no one who violates the fundamental principle in the manner you have described will ever enter my kingdom lest they be forgiven by me. And, I can assure you that without substantial mitigating factors, forgiveness would not come easy. Anyone else?"

"Yes, anyone who seeks to profit by claiming to speak for you. I mean, I don't have anything against churches, but do their buildings have to be that fancy. I also see many church leaders drive fancy cars and wear fancy clothes and it's obvious they do so because of the money that they collect in your name from those who believe are giving their money to you. I think that is really low and slimy. I think anyone profiting from claiming to speak for you is guilty of mass violations of the fundamental principle 'cause they are misleading many to part with their money. That's just plain wrong!"

"I know exactly who you mean. There's nothing holy about taking my children's money by making them believe that they are giving it to me. After all, I have never seen a penny from any of those speaking for me. Not that I need any of their money, but to see hardworking individuals part with their money in response to a plea from their clergy and then see that clergy use it to benefit himself is very disturbing to me. Pretending to speak for me is not meant to be a way to enrich yourself. Is there anyone else?"

"I've been thinking about where we live, Lord. You gave us a great place to live and thrive and all some people can do is to make as much money as they can and not care about how they affect our home. Man places such a high importance in money that he is willing to sacrifice our air, water, and well-being just so they can maximize their profit. Pretty soon we aren't going to have a place to live. Do you know what I mean, Lord?"

"I know exactly what you mean. When someone jeopardizes the air, water, and land of all my children for the sake of profit, it is a gigantic violation of the fundamental rights of all of the people on Earth. You are most insightful, Ricabar, considering you have spent most of your life indoor. The indigenous people of your country had it right when they saw themselves as stewards of the land they lived on. They felt humans needed to take only what was necessary to live without causing harm to the land. Unfortunately, modern man does not see it this way and looks only at the dollar when taking from the land. He does not care if his taking harms the air, water, or land so long as he is seeing dollars go in his pocket. Most distressing. Anyone else, Ricabar?"

Ricabar thought for a while and then said, "Yeah. All those who try to gouge us with their high prices for things like oil and gas, clothing and food. I think they take advantage of the fact that we need what they sell but they seem to charge way more than what their products are worth just so that they can make huge and obscene profits."

"Okay. I'm listening. Go on."

"Let me see," Ricabar said as he gazed up at the ceiling. "You know, I hate it when people try to take extreme shortcuts and try to get away with as much as they can just because they are impatient and don't want to wait or don't want to put in the effort and time to do it right. Do you know the type I'm talking about?"

"I think I have an idea of whom you speak, but perhaps you're going a little too far in targeting persons who simply have bad habits and their violations of the fundamental principle don't seem that egregious. Don't you think? It sounds to me that if you had your choice, you would include such people as those car drivers who, even though they see a sign telling them their lane is closed up ahead, they continue on until the lane finally ends and then try to maneuver carelessly over to the other lane because they simply don't want to wait in line. Would you include these people as well?"

Ricabar smiled and shook his head. "I suppose you're right. I am getting carried away. However, I would argue that anyone who has committed a serious violation of your fundamental principle should meet the same fate as I deserve. Of that much I'm certain."

"I can't disagree with you on that point, Ricabar. You've given me much to contemplate about and I will certainly give it my utmost consideration. You have done well with the brain I gave you. Perhaps we can talk later at length about your thoughts and ideas."

Without warning, the room abruptly became dark and Ricabar saw the Guest no more. "Wait, Lord. We haven't discussed a time frame or what comes afterwards. Come back, please," he pleaded but to no avail.

He extended his hand in the darkness to the area where the Guest had stood but felt nothing. Though he had been standing while speaking to the Guest, he suddenly found his body lying across on the bed and he was rubbing his eyes. He immediately raised his head and upper body off the bed and began breathing heavily. Did all of this happen or was I dreaming, he pondered as he scanned the room with his eyes. "But I don't remember falling asleep. When did that happen?" he asked out loud. Had this all been a dream, he wondered. He was beginning to feel a profound disappointment when he noticed something glowing around the door to his cell. He stared intently in that direction and quickly realized that something was entering through the gaps between the door and the frame which surrounded it. As he kept his eyes on the door, he saw that it was a glowing mist and it was beginning to filter throughout the room. Ricabar immediately figured out what it was and smiled. He gently laid down on his bed and looked straight up.

"Thank you, Lord. I'll see you soon." Ricabar said and maintained his smile as the glowing mist permeated the entire cell and his life on Earth was no more.